The Box Top to
Life's Puzzle

The Box Top to
Life's Puzzle

*Examining life's mystery from a
distinctive perspective*

MARCUS HURST

Copyright © 2017 by Marcus Hurst.

ISBN: Hardcover   978-1-5245-9190-8
                     Softcover   978-1-5245-9189-2
                     eBook   978-1-5245-9188-5

All rights reserved. No part of this book may be reproduced or transmitted in any form or by any means, electronic or mechanical, including photocopying, recording, or by any information storage and retrieval system, without permission in writing from the copyright owner.

Scripture quotations are from the ESV® Bible (The Holy Bible, English Standard Version®), copyright © 2001 by Crossway, a publishing ministry of Good News Publishers. Used by permission. All rights reserved.

Any people depicted in stock imagery provided by Thinkstock are models, and such images are being used for illustrative purposes only.
Certain stock imagery © Thinkstock.

Print information available on the last page.

Rev. date: 03/16/2017

To order additional copies of this book, contact:
Xlibris
1-888-795-4274
www.Xlibris.com
Orders@Xlibris.com
753989

1

Life's Puzzle

Is there nothing for us as humans to get out of life? What is the meaning of life anyhow? We are born, we live a little while, and then we die. Is that all? Is there nothing for us humans to get out of life? How do we know how to live and what to do if we don't have the big picture?

These are longstanding questions that have been plaguing humanity for thousands of years. For instance, nearly three thousand years ago, a king named Solomon reigned in Jerusalem. Solomon was known all over the ancient world for his exceptional riches and his astounding wisdom, and even *he* had these questions.

Solomon recorded a detailed description of his search for answers in a book titled Ecclesiastes. Following is excerpts

1

from the second chapter of this book, translated into the English language.

> I searched with my heart how to cheer my body with wine . . . and how to lay hold on folly, till I might see what was good for the children of man to do under heaven during the few days of their life. I made great works. I built houses and planted vineyards for myself. I made myself gardens and parks, and planted in them all kinds of fruit trees. I made myself pools from which to water the forest of growing trees . . .
>
> I had also great possessions of herds and flocks, more than any who had been before me in Jerusalem . . . Also my wisdom remained with me. And whatever my eyes desired I did not keep from them . . .
>
> Then I considered all that my hands had done and the toil I had expended in doing it, and behold, all was vanity and a striving after wind, and there was nothing to be gained under the sun.

Doesn't this sound familiar? Isn't this the same conclusion many people come to today? And even a famously wise man like Solomon, who had everything money could buy him, had no better answer than "There was nothing to be gained under the sun."

Like Solomon, countless people are devoting their life to the pursuit of wealth, a good reputation, and various forms of self-indulgence in hopes of finding a sustaining sense of fulfillment. Although these things can bring enjoyment, at best, it is but an empty form of pleasure, always craving for more and never content to just relax and be satisfied.

Many folks try to avoid quietness and inactivity in a subconscious attempt to prevent thinking about their ongoing pursuit of satisfaction and self-worth. Even so, millions battle with depression and a sense of worthlessness. In fact, this is an underlying cause behind much of today's drug abuses and suicides. Meanwhile, this quest for fulfillment is pushing criminal activity to a dangerous height.

The reality of these facts brings on the question, "Is there an answer? Is there nobody that has a better conclusion than Solomon's?"

Fortunately, there *is* an ultimate explanation, but first we need to prepare to accept it.

2

A Look at Truth

How do we know what is true? Numerous explanations for these questions are circulating, and each of them claims to be accurate. Therefore we will first look at truth.

We do best to maintain an open mind to the truth. Nothing is as secure as confidently standing on the solid ground of reality, and nothing is as repulsive as struggling through the swamp of falsehoods and error.

Now, it turns out, that the only ground on which truth is embraced is on the ground of humility. You see, proud people will generally consider their own opinion of higher value than the truth. It is a game of proud people to attempt at explaining away every fact they do not want to face. This can leave them, and those influenced by them, with a very distorted image of life and its values.

The Box Top to Life's Puzzle

If we do not like the truths we find, instead of trying to find a way around them, we do best to face them anyway. Where I live in central Pennsylvania, there is no shortage of winding roads and sharp curves. But suppose one day, when I am in a big hurry, I choose to believe that a certain windy road is straight and I can drive really fast. I would have to get another car; for even if I managed to persuade myself that the road is straight, it will still have every curve that it had before. I can effectively ignore that fact, but it will be to my downfall.

Truth stands, whether it is believed or not. Avoiding it is always going to be a cruel and disappointing road to travel. Nevertheless, to embrace reality, one needs to be humble, and being humiliated is uncomfortable in all parts of the world.

It really is hard to keep our minds open to a viewpoint that contradicts the one we hold as correct. No one likes being told that the view they support is wrong; nevertheless, if we hold conflicting opinions and are both convinced we are right, it is obvious that someone who is sure they are right is going to be wrong.

Did it ever happen to you, that you were sure you were correct and then someone showed you that you were wrong after all? This happened to me in number of times.

For this reason, a man of true wisdom will maintain doubts about his own opinions. That generally is a big job; overconfidence in our viewpoints is very easy. But if we do not maintain an open mind, we can so quickly be stuck in a ditch far from the truth. Everybody makes mistakes, but it takes a strength of character to admit them and pursue the correct alternative.

You may wonder, "is there any way to know what the truth is?"

Yes, when a humble and open-minded person comes across a truth, they will acquire confidence of its truthfulness. Do not get this confused with the smug confidence a proud person will have, which feels similar but tends to be totally inaccurate. Consider this proverb, "The confidence of the humble is true; while the certainty of the proud is an error."

Despite all this, a display of evidence will never convince those who are not willing to believe it. For this reason, if you are not open to a different opinion than you already believe, then reading this book may greatly aggravate you. In any case, please keep in mind, even if you want to believe a lie, you are only deceiving yourself; the truth will still be the truth. Barry Levefall said, "There are none who are as deaf as those who do not want to hear."

In these first two chapters, we have looked at the puzzle pieces scattered all over the table. We have seen what life is like when the big picture is not consulted, and we have considered the importance of accepting the truth even if it

There are none who are as deaf as those who do not want to hear.
—Barry Levefall

is scary. Now, let us take a dose of humility have a look at the story of the box top.

When one reaches a state of true humility, he will find it much more relaxing than the high maintenance of pride. In the end, living a humble life is much more enjoyable. C. S. Lewis put it well when he said, "Pride is the chief cause of misery in every nation." (Just a note, when pride is mentioned throughout this book, it is always referring to an excessive form of self-esteem.)

I only want to present the truth, no matter how hard it is to accept. But I do not guarantee that one hundred percent of this information is accurate. You may greatly question some of the ideas presented, and I do not doubt that I would question them too if they were new thoughts for me. I invite you to check these things out for yourself whether they be so.

Introducing the layout of this book

The explanations for life and the universe trace their roots to two parent views, evolution and creation.

Evolutionist believe our universe and everything in it, is the fruit of a string of random changes that, over billions of years, brought all these things to their existing form. Although the idea of evolution is much newer then that of creation, much of the professional world believes it. In fact, evolution has been broadly accepted as an indisputable fact, and is widely taught in education systems across the world.

Creationist believe that an almighty super-being brought the entire universe into existence in six days by merely giving the command. The idea of creation is as old as history. Although this viewpoint is despised by many as ignorance and fantasy, a number of folks still hold to it as an indisputable fact.

Still other people prefer to hold various hybrids of evolution and creation as a fact.

I have personally taken a thorough look at these viewpoints and have arrived to a conclusion. In the following chapters, we will explore this final conclusion and the evidences that have lead me to it.

3

The Global Acceptance
of a Lie

Over the years, numerous leaders and professionals rejected the common explanations for many of man's questions and have applied their own reasoning.

Why did they do this?

Due to pride and self-confidence, these folks had a burning desire to think as they please. For this reason, they determined that it would be more convenient to fabricate their own stories.

First, they came up with the theory of evolution, which accommodates the idea that supernatural authorities have never existed, then they chose to believe it and proceeded to inform the world that it was the truth. This led to a wide acceptance of naturalism, and a denial of the existence of miracles . . .

We know this may sound absurd, especially if you have been led to believe that evolution is a reasonable fact. Even so, if a truth sounds ridiculous, that doesn't change the fact that it is true. Evolution had to sound ridiculous too when it was first introduced. But folks can believe almost anything if they desperately want to. They do this by holding up the facts they want to support and ignoring the facts they would rather not find,

> **Folks can believe almost anything, if they desperately want to.**

Before we continue, let us make it clear that most people may not exactly believe evolution for the reasons we state here. We understand that many people accept evolution simply because it is what they are taught in school and it is what most prominent people believe. Neither does the average person have the backbone to stand up against it (due to its wide acceptance) if they do happen to question its accuracy. Nevertheless, the reasons we state here were the underlying motives behind the acceptance of this theory.

It was not hard to get people to believe evolution, because it was what people wanted to hear. It was what they wanted to hear because they had a passionate craving for the freedom to do as they please, and this craving greatly weakened their respect for the truth.

Now that they believe that supernatural powers do not exist, folks take pleasure in basking in their supposed liberty.

They especially relish the assumed freedom of not being under a moral law. You see, the evolution story conveniently does not include the evolution of an instinctive moral code. If one believes evolution, there is no moral code to observe. For this reason, folks who believe evolution believe that humans are on the same moral level as animals. Suddenly, the only thing that makes a particular action wrong is if the local government does not allow it.

The next step was to beg the government for a slacker set of moral laws. That was not hard either; government officials liked the idea too. And WHOOPY! If one believes evolution, he is theoretically out from under a moral code; as far as morality is concerned, he can feel increasingly more liberated to do what he wants!

"What makes you reach such a rash conclusion?" you might wonder.

Following, are three main reasons I stand were I do. These are all explained in detail at later points.

1. Through my personal experiences with the supernatural.

2. The personal and public evidence/probability that the Holy Bible is the truth, (the story of creation is strictly from this book).

3. The extreme unlikelihood of evolution, made apparent by honest evaluations.

I also take smaller details into consideration, which are all covered in this book as well.

Amazingly, the rejection of moral obligations and the wide spread pursuit of one's personal desires, are a fulfillment of a two-thousand-year-old prophecy found in the second book of Timothy, in the third chapter, where it is recorded:

> But understand this, that in the last days there will come times of difficulty. For people will be lovers of self, lovers of money, proud, arrogant, abusive, disobedient to their parents, ungrateful, unholy, heartless, unappeasable, slanderous, without self-control, brutal, not loving good, treacherous, reckless, swollen with conceit, lovers of pleasure rather than lovers of God… always learning and never able to arrive at a knowledge of the truth. (verses 1–4, 7)

Despite what proud people have to say (we already saw that their opinion cannot be trusted), supernatural authorities do exist! These powers are commonly referred to as *God* (the original and unrestricted), and *Satan* (the devil).

God is the ultimate authority. He has supreme power over everything and everybody, and He is the mastermind behind the universe and every form of life. God deeply loves each of us as if there were only one of us! He is exceptionally patient and is quick to forgive any lamented offense upon a humble request.

On the other hand, Satan is the source of hatred, confusion, and cruelty, and he desperately craves the discomfort and destruction of all humanity. Satan is the instigator that has led folks to this independent attitude, and upon getting a grip on his victims, he will proceed in distorting their reasoning, training them to accept his lies, avoid the truth, and become faithful helpers in his dark kingdom.

4

"Is That Really True?"

You may be thinking, "Do you really think God and Satan exist? You said God has supreme authority. If that is so, why doesn't He remove evil from His earth and shut Satan down?"

Good questions. We'll start with the first one.

Do you really think God and Satan exist?

To start with, we know rain exists, for most of us have experienced rain and have seen its effects. If someone were to tell us that rain is merely a character in a fairy tale and never actually was, we would know without a hesitation, that they are wrong. We have often seen rain, we likely have gotten wet by rain, and many of us have seen flooding as an obvious effect of rain. There is no doubt in our minds that rain is a reality.

In the same way, I know God and Satan exist.

Of myself, this book would have never materialized. It was God that got after me to write it and patiently walked me through the countless hours of it. (That is why, throughout this book, I refer to the author as *we.*) For example, as I type this, it is 10:40 PM. At 10:00 I was in bed, and it was

It was God that got after me to write this book and patiently walked me through the countless hours of it.

God that distinctly put in my mind to get up and work on this project. It was He who gave me the assurance that He would give me some important thoughts to write down.

I did not feel like getting up, but God persisted. So I got out of bed, sat down at my desk; and upon opening this writing project, the following note caught my eye: *Explain how I am confident that God and Satan exist.*

It was God that put this explanation into my mind, and it is Him that keeps me supplied with a steady stream of words as I type. He also just spelled out, in my mind, the word *steady,* when the spelling did not come on its own. Ultimately, I have worked very closely with God, through the writing of this book, to bring it to its current configuration.

For the last years, I have kept a journal of some of the more significant acts of God that I have personally experienced. Following, we have included two of its twenty-four entries.

February 19, 2016. I was driving home from Red Rock Refuge for a weekend off when I thought of it that I had forgotten my wallet and my car was nearly out of gas. Upon consideration and prayer, I decided to keep on going; I had enough gas to get home, and although I do not keep cash on hand at home, I figured it was God's will and I would manage.

I had something to drop off for a friend when I get home again, so I stopped in there on my way home. While there, his dad handed me $120 in cash for a past service I had done for them! At home I found a $525 check for me in the mail, and two mysterious piles of cash on my dresser totaling up to $100, with notes attached that indicated they were for services I had done for the neighbors five or more years ago! (My mother found them in my father's desk.) I find God really does take care of His people!

October 28, 2016. This evening, on my journey home, I watched the voltage level slowly diminish on the voltage gauge of my car. I acknowledged there was a good chance I would not make it home.

As the battery voltage decreased, I shut off as many lights and accessories as possible to preserve battery life. Every so often, my mental fingers would cross, and I would pry them apart and tell myself that if God would be satisfied with me in the ditch, then I would try to be too.

When I was getting close to home, the headlights barely shone anymore and vehicles would pull out in front of me like I wasn't there. I had the turning signal on to turn in at our house when it stopped ticking! I was able to coast to a stop right where my car belongs! I said to myself, "I would certainly not have made it much farther! But then, what was there to worry about anyhow? For, of a certainty, God was in control!"

I am confident that God's presence is always a fact.

--------◆◆◆◆◆◆--------

On the other hand, I have ample proof that Satan despises this book. He did his best to distract me and discourage me from completing it.

It was he who kept causing a horrible mental sensation, to come over me when I worked on my writing projects this past winter, in an attempt to make me give up. He would have succeeded with his mission if God had not heard my cry for deliverance and got him to stop it.

It is Satan that keeps placing bad thoughts into my mind at strategic moments in hopes that I dwell on them and let them lure me away from my relationship with God.

I also have discovered, during the time I spent at Red Rock Refuge, that the residents behaved a lot better when I asked God to suppress Satan's influence.

These accounts might sound like they are made up. Nonetheless, they are actual experiences of mine, which I distinctly remember in much more detail than has been recorded.

If someone were to tell me that supernatural authorities are merely characters in ancient myths, I would know without hesitation that they are wrong. The influence of the supernatural is as real to me as the tongue in my mouth.

I have located only two ways a person can deny the existence of supernatural powers. These are, if their mind is closed to that idea, or if they never questioned the theory that they do not exist.

You may be desperately thinking, "Oh, I hope this isn't true. I really do not want to believe it." We know that if God does exist, and if He does have expectations of us, He must hate most of what we do.

God is the only comfort and our only possible ally. He is also the supreme terror, for we have made Him our enemy. A supreme authority is either a great safety or a great danger, depending on how one reacts to it, and many of us have reacted the wrong way.

It is put well in 2 Corinthians 4:4 where it is found, "The god of this world (Satan) has blinded the minds of the unbelievers, to keep them from seeing the light of the gospel of the glory of Christ, who is the image of God." And in Matthew 13:15, "For this people's heart has grown dull, and with their ears they can barely hear, and their eyes they have closed, lest they should see with their eyes and hear with their ears and understand with their heart and turn, and I (Christ) would heal them."

Clearly, this book was not written to accommodate the headstrong, but rather to enhance the life of those who humbly absorb the difficult principles therein, which have proven to be so revolting to the selfish soul.

Why doesn't God remove evil from His earth and shut Satan down?

Instead of running us like robots, God has chosen to give us the independence of making our own choices. He also has chosen to never choose for us.

Instead of running us like robots, God has chosen to give us the privilege of choice.

Consequently, evil is a result of our bad choice, and could be replaced with purity if we would choose to do so. On his own, man defaults to doing evil. It is only by God's help that a condition of "good" can be reached. As long as man is proud, and as long as he does not ask God for help, man *will* do evil!

God did not create evil, but He does allow the possibility of evil, so that we have the choice to support the evil or the good.

5

God, the Only Source

God created the entire universe. Last of all, He made man in His own likeness and gave him a charge to dress and keep the earth. In other words, our layout and programming is a duplicate of God's functionality. He is the top authority and reigns supreme; we, as humans, are the crown of His creation and have the responsibility of managing the earth while it remains.

God had a collection of sixty-six books written, to provide us with some of our history and to answer our questions concerning life and our role on earth. They also paint a reasonable picture of God's character and purposes. Today, these books have been put together in one book titled *The Holy Bible.*

Because the Bible does not accommodate pride and frequently condemns viewpoints that folks like to support, numerous people have endeavored to convince the public that it is false. However, to successfully accomplish this, they need to ignore the fact that the Bible has been proven to be scientifically, archeologically, prophetically, and medically accurate. In addition, it includes countless historical facts that secular history sources have confirmed.

Also, considering the fact that the Bible was written over the course of about 1500 years, through more than forty authors who were from three different continents; the different books have been proven to accommodate each other remarkably well. Although its destruction is repeatedly attempted, it is still the most widely read book in the world.

It is nearly (if not totally) impossible to read the Bible with an open mind and not be convinced of its authority and accuracy.

Originally there was no imperfection or form of negativity on the face of the earth. But the very first human couple took life into their own hands and made the first tracks down this corrupted road we walk on today.

Before his initial sin, man only knew what was good. But the minute he did evil, his eyes were opened, and he then knew evil along with the good. Therefore, God implanted a moral code in man's mind to help him discern between the evil and the good.

After man corrupted himself, God saw the need to increase man's workload to help keep him occupied so his mind would not be as quick to stray to places it should not be found. God also uses obstacles such as disease and death to teach, admonish and guide humanity.

God refuses to give up on us. Part of His plan for our deliverance was to place a feeling of futility and emptiness in the heart of all individuals who neglect to obey His will and do not credit Him His due position. He does this that they might gain consciousness of their error, and the awareness of a malfunction in their life. This dissatisfaction also unsettles people's lives, that they might be more interested in the lives of those they can see live more peacefully. This makes it possible for others to draw them closer to God.

God wants to have a relationship with us; therefore unless our relationship with Him is right, we will not have peace in our life. For this reason, God built into us, a need **Unless our relationship with God is right, we will not have peace in our life.** to worship. This need to worship is mandatory; if we fail to worship God, we *will* find a substitute.

Nevertheless, God allows us to feel complete only when we are dedicated to Him and allow Him to control our life. After all, due to His infinite knowledge, life always works better if we let God have complete control. Here is an example:

I did most of this writing in the later hours, between 9:00 and 11:00 PM. I found that if I stop writing and go to bed because it is getting late, I'll have an attitude at the alarm clock in the morning. In contrast, if I keep writing till my mind no longer functions properly, or until God puts into my mind that I can now go to bed, I'll wake up feeling marvelous.

This morning is a good illustration. I am writing this paragraph while I wait for breakfast, since I got up earlier than normal. Last night I was working on this project till 12:20 AM, then when I went to bed, my mind didn't shut down, and I needed to get back up to write down some notes concerning this very subject. It was 1:30 AM till I finally got to bed for the last time!

That's amazing, isn't it! It shows that if we let God have His way, even when it contradicts the way we think, we will be more satisfied in the end.

Like us, God enjoys being obeyed and respected. As long as we are pursuing things that God does not want us to have, we will lead a discontented and miserable life.

Wealth, influence, and living for self, cannot make people happy. Only God's smile on our life can bring us lasting tranquility and genuine peace of mind. With this, the poorest individual can be content and at peace. Without it, even the famed celebrity must be (at least inwardly) apprehensive and deficient.

Truthfully, the impulsive pursuits of man always lead toward a state of bondage. Satan likes to manipulate people's reasoning, to the point that many folks run headlong into bondage, looking for freedom. (For many people, this generally is not hard for Satan to accomplish, because they deny that he even exists.)

Here is an experience I personally, periodically encounter in my relationship with God:

When I become lax and get caught up in a selfish world of my own, a certain undesirable sensation of worry and anxiety comes sneaking over me. Through experience, I have found that my best line of action is to promptly renew my commitment to God. So I ask him to forgive me where I have failed and be with me as I face life's challenges. Instantly, I feel the presence of God upon me, and a wave of serenity surrounds me! My burden is lifted, and I go on my way rejoicing!

Although we have the power of choice, we still have a very limited picture of what we are to accomplish in life.

Therefore, it is God's plan for us to depend on Him and His Bible for personal guidance and the instructions we need to accomplish His will.

In the Bible, God has promised to always be there for us and to never let us down. He will never turn a deaf ear to our concerns and is always there to hear us out and help us through the problems of life. (We cover more about communication with God in a later chapter.)

I know, it frequently appears likes God has blown these promises. But I am finding for myself that this is merely an illusion, a story Satan is parading in front of us in hopes that we stop trusting God.

Sometimes God's will is so different then what we have in mind, that we cannot see why He would desire things to happen that way. It helps if we think of ourselves as tools in His hands. We need to repeatedly say, "Your will be done." Then we need to take a deep breath, and do whatever He asks of us.

Truly, life makes little sense if God is acknowledged; but when the existence of God is accepted, the pieces come together and suddenly the big picture is made visible.

God's people

People who devote their life to God (which includes maintaining a close relationship with Him, and endeavoring to do His will) are commonly referred to as Christians.

Spectators in the first century gave them this name when they observed their unwavering devotion to Christ. (For any who might not know who Christ is, an explanation is coming in chapter eight.)

The name *Christian*, however, is used much more casually today. Many people who consider themselves Christians are not Christians by the Bible's standards. In many situations, numerous modern Christians no longer teach Bible truths as literal facts. This slowly increases over time, when Christians become slack and begin to accept Satan's suggestions as to how to interpret the Bible. (I say this very carefully.)

Many Christians hold to the Christian religion because that's what their parents believed, and deep in their heart they feel it is right. But, they resist the idea of letting God have control of their life, and except for Christian rituals and honoring their churches "standards," they mostly live their like anybody else would.

Due to these facts, many folks have a very distorted picture of what Christianity really is. This fact alone has been instrumental in causing many people to reject this religion.

For these reasons, we consider it important to note that in the following chapters, when we refer to Christians, we are referring only to people who exercise an unwavering dedication and unquestioning obedience to Christ.

6

Satan, Full of Destruction

It is commonly believed that Satan lived with God and was His chief assistant. Despite this, Satan got proud and tried to make himself equal to God. (His pride was the birth of all evil and rebellion.) Due to his rebellion, God cast Satan out of heaven.

Satan hates God and all God's people. Since that event Satan hated God and all God's people. Therefore he likes to get us to believe many lies and negative thoughts concerning them to scare us away and distract us from seeing the obvious blessings that come along with being God's people. Nevertheless, although Satan is very powerful and influential, God is all-powerful and will always maintain authority over Him.

The following are some thoughts that Satan is likely to parade before the minds of skeptical readers to distract them

28

from the blessings of God. He does this that he might avoid the pain of seeing a happy person. After each thought from Satan, we have included the truth concerning that matter.

―――――― ✦✦✦✦✦ ――――――

Thought from Satan: "All these notions are out of the Bible, and the Bible isn't true."

The truth is, as we have mentioned earlier, if one reads the Bible with an open mind (especially the New Testament), it is impossible to not feel the power of its contents. The spirit of God truly abounds in its pages and speaks through its words.

For myself, when I consult my Bible, it often opens to a scripture that especially speaks to me. Frequently, that scripture mentions the urgency of educating unwary people about God and His requirements for those that seek to follow him.

The idea that the Bible is false is eagerly accepted by many because they like the idea of getting out from under its authority.

―――――― ✦✦✦✦✦ ――――――

Thought from Satan: "Look at all your problems! Nobody cares about your well-being. That's all a smooth tale!"

The truth is, in reality, many of our problems come from wanting our own way, and many more come from having it. God sees the whole picture of our life and is much more capable of knowing what is best for us. His plan for us, in all prospects, is better than our plan for ourselves.

The rest of the obstacles we face in life are allowed by God because He does care deeply about us. He wants us to go through those experiences to fine-tune our character to what He wants of it and to steer us down the path he wants us to go.

The experiences and problems we face also double as a test to see how we handle each situation. When we whine and balk, we are underestimating God and His divine plan for us, and are only multiplying our problems. We would feel much better about life's disappointments if we promptly accept them as God sent adjustments to our course.

———————————— ✦✦✦✦✦ ————————————

Thought from Satan: "Christianity is fanatical. What would your friends think of you?"

The truth is, maintaining a healthy relationship with God will significantly enhance anybody's life and is far more fulfilling than any other relationship one could have. When one is living a much more satisfactory life, he is not likely to be concerned about negative thoughts his friends might be entertaining concerning him. More likely he would be asking them to join him.

———————————— ✦✦✦✦✦ ————————————

Thought from Satan: "Christians can't have any fun. A Christian lifestyle must certainly be boring with such ridged moral standards and all the other restrictions that go with it!"

The truth is, becoming a Christian would remove a heavy load from your heart and mind. This will result in profound peace and an uncontainable joy that God freely grants to those who take time for Him. this will by far repay the efforts and difficulties one may face for being a Christian.

God makes sure His people never regret any effort they make to support Him. Often by showering them with profound satisfaction and peace of mind and the knowledge that He is with their efforts. One will find that life is much more satisfactory when they restrain themselves from those self-indulgences that many folks call fun.

Every part of us was designed to live righteously. People are not content because they are not practicing righteousness and right living, they are not living right because Satan is in control of their life. In contrast, Christians will want to pursue upright living. Christians have a loving God in control of their life instead of a wrathful devil. Therefore as long as they pursue God's will, they will be content.

As for the restrictions: let's have a story.

Once there was a small girl who was hungry for something to eat. She found one of those neatly decorated bars of soap that looks a lot like a big piece of candy! It smelled good too!

This girl decided she would like to take a bite! About this time, her mother saw what was about to take place and she snatched the soap from her just in time!

That little girl was not very happy, and she didn't get happier after her mother told her that it would not taste as good as it looks. She said to herself, "I want to eat that big piece of candy! Mom just called it soap so I don't eat it!"

And after some thinking, she concluded, "I don't like being told what to do. I want to do whatever I feel like."

The next week, this girl finds the same bar of soap. This time she gets her wish and takes a big bite!

"Oh!" she said, "Mom was right after all! It *is* soap!"

It does us good to consider that the restrictions God gives His people are for their own benefit. We will feel much better about these restrictions if we humbly submit to them, even if we don't understand their purposes.

Though we will crave the prohibited at times, it does us good to practice self-control. It doesn't pay to get arrogant and ignore the rules and end up with a mouthful of soap.

———— ✦✦✦✦✦ ————

Thought from Satan: "You don't have time for God or religion."

The truth is, naturally, one will always find time for the things they want to do. Sincere Christians want to take time for God and

His work, and they find deep satisfaction and enjoyment in doing so. The more time we take for God, the closer our relationship grows with Him and the more we will understand His purposes.

———— ✦✦✦✦✦✦ ————

God and Satan are constantly placing thoughts in our mind, much like billboard advertising. But we would like to verify that we, as creatures of choice, have the ability and authority to accept or reject any of these thoughts.

Some folks may find Satan's advertising too compelling, and they find it almost impossible to resist. Yes, Satan is a very skilled tempter, and he knows in which areas we are most likely to yield. It is only with God's help that we can overcome. "With man this is impossible, but with God all things are possible" (Matthew 19:26).

I found for myself that God does very well at helping me win these mental battles with Satan if I only ask Him to. The Bible also promises, "No temptation has overtaken you that is not common to man. God is faithful, and he will not let you be tempted beyond your ability, but with the temptation he will also provide the way of escape, that you may be able to endure it" (1 Corinthians 10:13).

Nothing beats the satisfaction of experiencing God's smile of approval upon your life! Of a truth, one will never regret standing up against Satan and obeying God.

7

Evolved or Created?

Thought from Satan: "Everyone knows that the universe came into existence through an evolutionary process! How dare this scoundrel deny that fact! It's impossible for billions of people to be so wrong!"

Many of evolutions points appear highly fictional to the Christian's eye. However, many people feel the same way about the Christian's viewpoints. This fact tells us we cannot rely on mere feelings and emotions; these have no concern for the truth and are easily influenced by Satan.

––––––– ✦✦✦✦✦ –––––––

We all know how buildings and all the devices we use today are brought into existence. Man, through a demand of their use, thought up their design; and through much planning and precise modification and placement of natural product he caused them to exist.

But supposedly, the existence of the earth and all the outlaying bodies of the universe just happened by random chance, over billions and billions of years! For some reason, although all man-made things unquestionably require a mastermind behind their existence. Yet the existence of the universe and life on Earth is largely believed to have existed from nothing, with no intelligent design, and for no reason. Even while it is obvious that these are by far more complex than any man-made device.

Is it logical to think that the necessary environment on Earth to sustain life is an accident? And what about the water cycle, the ability of the human mind to reason, and ultimately, the existence of life itself?

Naturally, we find it very hard to take a thorough and honest look at something we have no interest in. Jonathan Swift, a writer from England, wrote, "Reasoning itself is true and just, but the reasoning of every particular man is weak and wavering, perpetually swayed and turned by his interest, his passions and his vices." There is much evidence for creation that many people choose to ignore because it is not what they want to look at.

Following are three examples of these evidences.

First, how is it that we can identify laws of nature that *never* change? The strangeness of the universe being so reliable has struck many great scientists. There is no logical necessity for our universe to obey rules, let alone abide by the rules of mathematics.

This astonishment sources from the recognition that the universe doesn't have to behave this way. Richard Feynman, a Nobel Prize winner for quantum electrodynamics, said, "Why nature is mathematical is a mystery . . . The fact that there are rules at all is a kind of miracle."

Second, all instruction is with intent. Instruction manuals are written with purpose. Did you know that the DNA in each human cell functions as a three-billion-letter instruction manual that tells the cell to act in a certain way?

One must ask, "How did this information wind up in each human cell?" These are not just chemicals. These are chemicals that code, in a very detailed way, exactly how the person's body should develop. Natural, biological causes are completely lacking as an explanation. You cannot find precise instruction like this without someone intentionally constructing it.

Thirdly, most things that people believe evolved by random chance, are more vast and complex than anything man has created. Can random chance really produce things of higher complexity than can be designed by intelligent beings?

Another thought: what is it about atheists that they put so much effort into disproving something that they don't believe even exists? Could the underlying reason for atheists being bothered by people believing in God be that God is actively pursuing them?

Malcolm Muggeridge, socialist and philosophical author, wrote, "I had a notion that somehow, besides questing, I was being pursued." C. S. Lewis said he remembered "whenever my mind lifted, even for a second, from my work, I felt the steady, unrelenting approach of Him whom I so earnestly desired not to meet."

--- ✦✦✦✦✦ ---

"Wait!" an evolutionist might exclaim, "Is there not substantial evidence that the Earth is more than six thousand years old like creationists claim? There is a whole list of evidence for evolution!"

Most of the facts that are thought of as evidence for evolution, can just as easily be interpreted as evidence for creation. Doesn't this occurrence void the supposed evidence of these facts?

Also, people who believe evolution tend to forget that creation believing folks also believe the Bible, and the Bible says, "With God all things are possible" (Matthew 19:26). If there is a supernatural intelligence that can work miracles, then this supernatural intelligence could have done anything, anywhere, in any way he wanted to. Thus, any supposed evidence for evolution may have been a miracle from a creation standpoint.

The Verdict

The often-shocking, yet honest, conclusion of the matter is, evidence for evolution is virtually nonexistent; it is merely imagined.

When one starts considering the idea of an existing God and a young earth, the evidences which are so desperately hidden by atheist become obvious.

Men dreamed up evolution (with Satan's assistance) in a desperate attempt to find a substitute idea for a fact folks no longer wanted to face. People do not believe in evolution because they have been led there by solid evidence. They are lured there by superficial, emotional, and personal factors.

Enthusiastically believing a lie never changed the truth about it, no matter how strongly the lie was believed.

Even if billions of people assume evolution to be an indisputable fact, that doesn't mean it is true. It only means that billions of people are either intentionally blind to the truth, or have never questioned the theory.

Enthusiastically believing a lie never changed the truth about it, no matter how strongly the lie was believed. If one is willing to take an honest look, he will discover that the theory of evolution is scientifically bankrupt. Alternatively, evidence for creation is strong, beyond a reasonable doubt. If these two opinions were tried in court with standard investigation processes, the idea of creation would be pronounced as the obvious truth.

It is only by deliberate blindness on the part of its enthusiasts, and a blind following of the blind on the part of society, that evolution is even considered possible.

Although an atheist will likely have some bad feelings concerning this book, we are not offended. We feel the same way when atheists downgrade our viewpoints. We did not write these offensive things about evolution because we are angry or because we so desperately despise the theory. We wrote them because we sincerely feel they are true.

Anybody who cares to challenge these facts is invited to take honest consideration and do their own research, to see for themselves if these things are so. We do want to abstain from leading anybody away from the truth.

8

What Happens When We Die?

We have already concluded that the Bible is God's word to man and consists of pure truths. It is frequently repeated in the Bible that God has appointed a time when the earth will burn up (2 Peter 3:10). The dead shall rise (1 Thessalonians 4:15), and there will be a great judgment in which God will judge each individual according to their deeds (Romans 2:5-6), revealing and publicly proclaiming every truth concerning them (Luke 12:3). The Bible also records that only God knows when this will happen (Matthew 24:35-42).

Folks who take life into their own hands and disregard God's will, must be condemned to an endless sentence with the devil and his servants in a pit that burns with an unquenchable flame and consists of every evil imaginable

(Mark 9:41). "The wicked shall be turned into hell, [and] all the nations that forget God" (Psalms 9:17, KJV).

The righteous people, whom God has forgiven and who have endeavored to comply to His standards, will be welcomed to live in the presence of God forever, in a state of perfect contentment.

"For the Lord himself will descend from heaven with a cry of command, with the voice of an archangel, and with the sound of the trumpet of God. And the dead in Christ will rise first. Then we who are alive, who are left, will be caught up together with them in the clouds to meet the Lord in the air, and so we will always be with the Lord" (1 Thessalonians 4:16, 17).

Life is but a temporary assignment. The problems we experience in this life help to remind us that Earth is not our ultimate home.

A Demand for Justice

You may be thinking, "Hell is cruel. Wouldn't it make better sense for God to destroy those who don't believe, if He is a loving God, instead of tormenting them?"

God is all-knowing and a God of perfect justice, He is also very thorough in revealing Himself to the open mind. Because God is all-knowing, He will not send anybody to hell that is innocent in any way; and since He is just, evil will not go unpunished. It would not be sufficient justice for God to kill His enemies.

It would make sense in our minds if God just saved everybody. But how? Against their will? Some people would rather continue their rebellion than be reformed. So God says, "Have it your way. You can continue your rebellion, but you'll be quarantined, so you can't pollute my perfect heaven." Besides, would it be sensible for God to send folks who cannot get along with Him, to a place where they'll be in His physical presents for an eternity?

We are not out to just scare people with hell, like some might suppose. We just want people to know the truth. For myself, I would rather not believe what the Bible says about hell, but I do want to face reality.

In the end, it is the existence of heaven and hell that gives meaning to life. Without them, our choices, our pleasures, our sufferings, and the lives of us and our loved ones would ultimately mean nothing. We would struggle through this life for no good reason. Without heaven and hell, this incredibly designed universe is a stairway to nowhere.

An atheist might conclude, "This life *is* a stairway to nowhere."

Well, if you do not want to believe the Bible and the truth therein, that is your choice. As we have mentioned before, nobody can change what you believe, if you are unwilling to

THE BOX TOP TO LIFE'S PUZZLE 43

change. We are only trying to present you the truth, but you certainly don't have to believe it if you don't want to.

God demands justice, but because of His great love for the corrupted human race, He set up a plan to liberate humanity, that they might experience complete forgiveness for their foolishness.

Therefore, about the year 5 BC, God caused a virgin woman to conceive (Luke 1:34-35). The child, Jesus (who was also called Christ), was a long-promised Savior to help people rise above their vices and give them a chance to start over.

Jesus experienced all the problems and temptations man faces, but He never sinned. However, His own people rejected Him; and because they were envious of His popularity, they had Him crucified. The following is inserts of this account from the Bible:

> So when they had gathered, Pilate said to them, "Whom do you want me to release for you: Barabbas, or Jesus who is called Christ?" For he knew that it was out of envy that they had delivered him up.
>
> They said, "Barabbas." Pilate said to them, "Then what shall I do with Jesus who is called

Christ?" They all said, "Let him be crucified!" And he said, "Why, what evil has he done?" But they shouted all the more, "Let him be crucified!"

Then he released for them Barabbas, and having scourged Jesus, delivered him to be crucified. Then the soldiers of the governor took Jesus into the governor's headquarters, and they gathered the whole battalion before him. And they stripped him and put a scarlet robe on him, and twisting together a crown of thorns, they put it on his head and put a reed in his right hand.

And kneeling before him, they mocked him, saying, "Hail, King of the Jews!" And they spit on him and took the reed and struck him on the head. And when they had mocked him, they stripped him of the robe and put his own clothes on him and led him away to crucify him.

Two robbers were crucified with him, one on the right and one on the left . . . One of the criminals who were hanged railed at him, saying, "Are you not the Christ? Save yourself and us!"

But the other rebuked him, saying, "Do you not fear God, since you are under the same sentence of condemnation? And we indeed justly, for we are receiving the due reward of our deeds; but this man has done nothing wrong." (Excerpts from Matthew 27 and Luke 23)

Three days after they crucified Jesus, He miraculously arose from the dead! (Matthew 28:1-7). In conquering his own death, Jesus has proven his ability to dismiss our penalty of damnation.

In the book of Ezekiel, it is recorded: "As I live, declares the Lord GOD, I have no pleasure in the death of the wicked" (33:11). Thanks to God's great mercy; it was His plan that His own Son (who was the only person to live a perfect life) would be tortured and crucified to take the place of the deserved punishment of all other individuals. "For one will scarcely die for a righteous person—though perhaps for a good person one would dare even to die—but God shows his love for us in that while we were still sinners, Christ died for us" (Romans 5:7, 8).

Jesus became sin for us. Although He was sinless Himself, He took the blame for the sins of humanity, that we might be ransomed.

"But," you might say, "I am a good person."

Perhaps you are good compared to some folks. Nevertheless, ever since man's initial disobedience, sin is the condition of every human heart. You are not good enough by God's standard, for God requires moral perfection.

Thanks to Christ, our lives can have meaning and none of us need to experience hell.

9

Spiritual Combat

All of us humans were born with the inclination to think and desire wrong things. First selfishness, then disobedience, pride, and dishonesty began to push their way into our life and control our being . . .

Babies are innocent of sin and are not accountable for their actions till they are old enough to understand what sin is. However, I think most of us have witnessed how infants tend to do those things that will be sin when they get older.

As we grow toward maturity, another force starts calling for our attention. This is God's spirit of love, peace, and goodness. The spirit of God (the Holy Spirit) knocks at the heart of every person who is old enough to make their own decisions. If we personally accept this spirit, it will make itself at home in our life.

God desires that humans personally choose to follow Him, over living the way of original inclinations. This way they are dedicated to doing His will, and in the long run, are more committed to Him.

If we would be born with God's spirit dominating our life, it likely would not be as precious to us, and we would find it easier to neglect devotion to it.

God desires His followers to have personally chosen to follow Him. This way they are dedicated to doing His will, and in the long run, are more committed to Him.

So here we are, influenced by the spirit of Satan and attracted by the spirit of God, which is tirelessly beckoning to us.

If we have seen the Holy Spirit at work in folks around us, we will be more likely to answer its calling and devote our life to it ourselves. Nevertheless, if we have never seen God's spirit function in the lives of our associates, we will likely follow their example. After all, is it not easier to buy something if we see it demonstrated?

Ultimately, we have a few routes before us from which to choose.

1. We can reject the wrong spirit and ask the Holy Spirit to rule in our lives. Then God shall grant us our wish and we can arise, renewed and ready for what God has in store for us.

   Satan will entice us to serve him instead. But if we have our mind set on God and are fully committed to Him, He is going to help us, and we shall win the battles. As our relationship with God grows, Satan is going to slink farther and farther away. However, he will never give up, and we shall battle this enemy until our death. Nevertheless, God will be with us, and we shall forever rejoice in our decision to follow Him.

2. We may decide to wait a while before making the decision. This is a dangerous option, for Satan will do his best to make sure there is no convenient time to change our allegiance. Also, we are not promised another day of opportunity.

   If we do decide to wait, God's spirit will long-sufferingly wait until we are ready to accept it.

3. If we are tired of being bothered and want to serve Satan without God reminding us of another way, we might desire God's spirit to go away and leave us alone. In this case, God's spirit will go away, and Satan shall

proceed to wrap his tentacles around us and drag us deeper and deeper into his dark kingdom.

Following is a few paragraphs from the book of Romans that accurately describes the situation in which Satan has gotten many people into:

> For although they knew God, they did not honor him as God or give thanks to him, but they became futile in their thinking, and their foolish hearts were darkened.
>
> Claiming to be wise, they became fools . . . Therefore God gave them up in the lusts of their hearts to impurity, to the dishonoring of their bodies among themselves, because they exchanged the truth about God for a lie and worshiped and served the creature rather than the Creator, who is blessed forever! Amen . . .
>
> And since they did not see fit to acknowledge God, God gave them up to a debased mind to do what ought not to be done. They were filled with all manner of unrighteousness, evil, covetousness, malice. They are full of envy, murder, strife, deceit, maliciousness. They are gossips, slanderers, haters of God, insolent, haughty, boastful, inventors of evil, disobedient

to parents, foolish, faithless, heartless, ruthless.
(Romans 1:21–22, 24–25, 28–31)

Although the path that looks the most inviting to man, leads to fear and hopelessness; God's way always leads to a satisfied mind, a substantial peace in one's life, and a joy in the soul.

10

Facing the Facts

Why would you remain a skeptic?

Perhaps you don't want to be humiliated and you are not sure about letting someone else have complete control of your life. This is an obstacle that every Christian had to face.

I remember when I was taking this step, my pride didn't want to be humiliated, and Satan desperately reminded me that he thought it was a cowardly thing to do. It was not easy to swallow my pride and ignore Satan's opinion. But the unspeakable joy that resulted, certainly was worth the effort! "For he satisfies the longing soul, and the hungry soul he fills with good things" (Psalm 107:9).

Life is like a huge maze. There are many attractive passages, and there is much controversy over which way is best. But our view is greatly limited and only God has the map and knows were each passage leads. Of ourselves, we will lose the way, only God can guide us to the desired location.

In some situations, humiliation is essential. Folks who are handicapped think it would be nice if they could help themselves. But that is not always an option. Many of them and find that they find that they need to submit to receiving aid, or die.

There is nothing progressive about being stubborn and refusing to admit a mistake. In the same way, we need to submit to receiving aid from God, in situations where we are unable to adequately help ourselves. God will not force himself on us, it will always be our choice. However, there is only one alternative, and if we do not choose Christ, that one *will* be forced on us.

If we were to find that we are on the wrong road, to experience progress, we would need to correct our mistake and find the right road. There is nothing progressive about being stubborn and refusing to admit a mistake.

Looking at the present state of the world, it is obvious that humanity has been making some big mistakes. We are on the wrong road, and facing that fact and making corrective adjustment to our course will be the quickest way to the right road.

Is it reasonable to doubt Christianity when we consider the evidence? In fact, considering the evidence, there is much reason to doubt any other explanation. We do well to trust that God knows what is best for us. We need to surrender our selfish will and embrace his perfect will.

Trust is essential if we are to surrender, and one will not surrender to a God they do not trust. Fear keeps us from trusting and surrendering, but "perfect love casts out fear," (1 John 4:18 NKJV). The more we realize how much God loves us, the easier it will be for us surrender to Him.

How do we know God loves us? The greatest expression of God's love for us, is the cruelty that Christ went through for our sakes. "but God shows his love for us in that while we were still sinners, Christ died for us." (Romans 5:8). When Christ was hanging on the cross, he was, in essence, saying, "I love you so much that I'd rather die than live without you."

God is not a cruel master that uses brute force to get us to submit to Him. He is a God of love and liberty. Surrendering to Him brings freedom, not bondage like Satan would have us believe. God is not an oppressor, but a liberator. He is not a dictator, but a friend.

11

Entering into God's Family

Another question you might have could be, "If this is true and God and Satan do exist, what should I do about it?"

If God exists, then the Bible is true. If the Bible is true, then humble yourself and read it. (Especially the latter part, the New Testament.) Then you need to take the truths you find in the Bible to heart and live accordingly. Relax and enjoy the box top to life's puzzle.

If you are thinking of becoming a Christian, we warn you. You are embarking on a mission that is going to take the whole of you. From God's viewpoint, there are no gray areas in Christianity. If one is not fully dedicated to Christ and totally open to His will, then they are not what God would consider a Christian.

The Christian religion is, in the long run, a thing of unspeakable comfort, but it does not begin in comfort. As previously mentioned, Christianity can only begin in complete humility. And it's no use trying to go on to that comfort without first going through that humility.

Comfort is one thing that cannot be gotten by looking for it. If we start by looking for and accepting the truth, we will find comfort in the end. However, if we start by looking for comfort, we will get neither comfort or truth, only a fleeting pleasure and wishful thinking to begin with and, in the end, despair.

How does an individual become a Christian and build a satisfying relationship with God?

You will need to adhere to the following:

1. Obtain humility. As we have mentioned before, humbleness can face the truth without resentment, and facing the truth is essential to any form of inner joy. We must accept that we are not the top dog in this world as we would like to think.

Being humble does not mean you need to walk around with a long face. The humility we are referring to is a meek submission to God's authority; it is the opposite of a self-righteous attitude. Humility is not for cowards, but for those that have enough backbone to face the truth as a can brave man.

2. Believe in God, and believe He has the power to forgive and forget your transgressions.

3. Ask God to forgive and forget your sins. Lay down your burdens before Him with the same confidence you have when you sit in your favorite chair. "If you confess with your mouth that Jesus is Lord and believe in your heart that God raised him from the dead, you will be saved," (Romans 10:9). God will only grant you your request if you sincerely believe He is going to, and then, He will. The only exception here is the fact that God will not forgive any sin that is not regretted.

To communicate with God, one needs only to think a thought. God knows all our thoughts, so if we process thoughts for Him to hear—whether spoken, whispered, or merely thought, He will understand. (Just so you know, God also understands thoughts that are not intended for Him to understand.)

Jesus says, "Come to me, all who labor and are heavy laden, and I will give you rest. Take my yoke upon you, and learn from me, for I am gentle and lowly in heart, and you will find rest for your souls. For my yoke is easy, and my burden is light" (Matthew 11:28–30). I am confident that God has been anticipating your acceptance of Him, and He will eagerly accept you into His family.

An unspeakable joy, which reflects from a complete absence of guilt and worry, is obtained when we lay down every burden and concern and let God have complete control of our life. "Therefore, if anyone is in Christ, he is a new creation. The old has passed away; behold, the new has come" (2 Corinthians 5:17). This blessed state cannot be earned or won but must be obtained only by asking for it and receiving it. Also, it can only be bestowed upon the fully devoted soul.

If you have asked God to forgive you, He has. Thank Him for it. Just like we humans, God likes to be praised and respected. I have found from experience, that some of the most satisfying feelings I have ever felt came when I was praising God.

In fact, worshiping God is a lifestyle that all Christians need to exercise. One can worship God through prayer and singing; however, these mean much more to God when our worship includes respectfulness and a life of dedication to His principles.

12

Living Life as a Christian

After taking the initial step, as described in the previous chapter, it is essential to build a personal relationship with God. This is done by communicating daily through prayer and earnestly studying the Bible and obeying it to our fullest ability. The way one converses with a friend as they work together is the way a Christian should pray to God throughout the day.

Food for the spiritual body (prayer, Bible study, and communication with other Christians) is as important for a Christian as food for the physical body.

Christians are commonly referred to as God's children, and to be a victorious child of God, a Christian will soon learn that he must not follow the common pattern of mankind. In fact, as a Christian, you will find that you no longer feel comfortable with the ways of common society but will only

59

feel at home in a sound Christian environment. For this reason, you will find it very beneficial to locate a sincere group of Christians to associate with. Christians function best in a group, where they can provide vital support for each other.

———————— ✦✦✦✦✦✦ ————————

Another aspect to living a Christian life is to live in constant humility and surrender to God's will. This is hard, it is not natural for humans to do, but it is possible if we seek God's assistance.

You can know you are surrendered to God when you rely on Him to work things out instead of trying to maintain control and insist on bringing about your personal will on your own strength.

You can know you have, at least a measure of, humility when you do not react to criticism by rushing to defend yourself, when you do not demand your rights, and when you can love and show respect to people even when they do not respect you.

Often, the hardest part to surrender to God is our money. We do well to trust in God instead of money, to supply us with peace of mind. We need to put money in its correct place by learning to enjoy giving it, instead of making a hobby out of collecting it.

THE BOX TOP TO LIFE'S PUZZLE 61

This level of surrender is hard work, but you will never catch yourself thinking that it was not worth it. As mentioned before, God will make sure you are rewarded for every effort you make to submit to His will.

So put Jesus Christ in the driver's seat of your life, and leave your hands off the steering wheel. Our week judgment and limited view can never compete with Christ's all-wise guidance.

We, as "heirs with Christ," if we are sincere, have the potential of influencing many of the world's actions and decisions, through intense, heartfelt prayer. "The prayer of a righteous person has great power as it is working. Elijah was a man with a nature like ours, and he prayed fervently that it might not rain, and for three years and six months it did not rain on the earth. Then he prayed again, and heaven gave rain, and the earth bore its fruit" (James 5:16–18).

It is because of the potential of a Christians heartfelt prayers, that Christians are taught to always pray with the attitude of "Thy will be done." Humanity's current corrupted state is a reality, because few people sincerely ask God for better conduct of man.

You may ask, "How do I know what God's will is for my life?"

If we openly seek God's will and maintain a close relationship with Him, He will reveal it to us. However, from experience I have found that God will not reveal His will to us before He wants us to know. Often, when I insist on knowing God's will for me ahead of time, I get this answer. "Calm down! I will let you know My will when it is My will for you to know it."

When we surrender our will to God, and willingly do what He desires of us, we are going to feel like we are in a team with God. We will be working, in a sense, side by side with the very one who created the universe!

Life is also much more fulfilling if one gets his mind off himself and starts being an aid to those around him. Living for the well-being of others will soon prove to be much more satisfying then living life solely for your own enjoyment.

———— ‧✦✦✦✦‧ ————

Can God help His people find victory over vices such as painful memories, fear and addictions?

Yes, although a Christian will find himself renewed, to the extent that he will not even feel like his old self, this does not mean their hardships will disappear overnight (although, some may have experienced that to a certain degree).

Still, as one of His children, a Christian will find that God does a great job at relieving the pain and comforting the soul. He can and will help His people rise above any obsession if they realize their own weakness and completely surrender their spirit to receiving His divine aid and guidance. "The angel of the Lord encamps around those who fear him, and delivers them" (Psalm 34:7). As breathing doesn't lower oxygen levels in the atmosphere and as waves never cease to wash ashore, so God's grace and mercy will never run dry!

No, Christianity is not effortless and easy. Yes, it requires much perseverance and prayer. No, Christianity is not effortless and easy. Yes, it requires much perseverance. Satan is visiting Christians constantly, trying to get them to compromise and lower their standards. He especially likes to get Christians to overlook the *small* issues and sins that supposedly are *not a big deal.*

If we as Christians are not on our guard and get careless, Satan will manipulate our thinking until it is no longer sound. Nevertheless, Christianity is truly worth the pain, for the security and contentment that can be had by it, far surpasses the insecure lifestyle that Satan has to offer.

A live body is not one that never gets hurt but one that can, to some extent, repair itself. In the same way, a Christian is not a man who never goes wrong but a man who is enabled, through the spirit of God, to repent, pick himself up and begin over again after each stumble.

We will never get to the end of growing in our Christian life, but ample rewards are reaped along the way.

To continue reading about living a Christian life, consider reading book *The Purpose Driven Life* by Rick Warren.

Author's Note

Following I have included a brief outline of the journey I took in writing this material.

I was thirteen years old when I swallowed my pride and made the life commitment to Christianity.

When I was about fourteen, the idea came to my mind to write a book that would answer some of the big questions that folks have about life. At first, I had the slightest idea were to start with this incredible work. I tried a few methods of presentation, but they did not work out; and soon the project was relocated to the back of my mind, in hopes that a marvelous idea for continuation happens along one day.

Then one day it happened! A wonderful idea for this project started brewing in my mind! I was ecstatic! Today, those original thoughts are located in the first and fifth chapters of this book. Over the next ten years, and between the production of half a dozen other writing projects, this manuscript went through dozens of molds and revisions.

This book was written from the depth of my heart, with the divine assistance of God Himself, and I feel assured that it has passed His inspection.

I was amazed, as I researched numerous sources, that our individual conclusions rarely contradicted each other. This is due to both of us getting our information from the Holy Spirit. This general accord helped me to mentally confirm the accuracy of my explanations.

If this book gives you any amount of spiritual help or answers, give God the praise. Of myself I could have done nothing.

Acknowledgement

God is the sole reason for this book. Its existence was His suggestion, and it was He who coaxed me through the whole process and encouraged me when I came to hard spots. I also worked closely with Him to come up with the needed points, many times just typing the words in as He placed them into my mind.

I can also give credit to a handful of friends who proofread and edited the manuscript, making their own suggestions as they saw fit. My parents and brothers sufficiently played the part of handing out opinions upon request.

Bibliography

Numerous thoughts throughout this book, were drawn from the following two books: *Mere Christianity* by C. S. Lewis, and *The Purpose Driven Life* by Rick Warren.

All scripture references are out of the English Standard Version of the Holy Bible, unless otherwise noted.

Other Books to Read

Here is a list of books that I suggest you should read as you overcome your doubts and grow in your Christian life.

I Don't Have Enough Faith to Be an Atheist by Norman L Geisler and Frank Turek

Mere Christianity by C. S. Lewis

God's Story, Your Story by Max Lucado

The Purpose Driven Life by Rick Warren

Doing What Comes Spiritually by John M. Drescher

Table of Contents

1. Life's Puzzle 1
2. A Look at Truth 4
3. The Global Acceptance of a Lie 9
4. "Is That Really True?" 14
5. God, the Only Source 21
6. Satan, Full of Destruction 28
7. Evolved or Created? 34
8. What Happens When We Die? 40
9. Spiritual Combat 47
10. Facing the Facts 52
11. Entering into God's Family 55
12. Living Life as a Christian 59

Author's Note 65
Acknowledgement 67
Bibliography 69
Other Books to Read 71

Printed in the United States
By Bookmasters